Knights, Maidens
and Dragons

Knights, Maidens and Dragons

SIX MEDIEVAL TALES OF VIRTUE AND VALOR

Retold by Julia Duin

To order additional copies of this book, contact:
Xlibris Corporation
1-888-795-4274
www.Xlibris.com
Orders@Xlibris.com

21554

Table of Contents

Dedicated to my mother,
who introduced me to the Little Colonel and
to my father, who still prays for my prince to come.

ACKNOWLEDGMENTS

These six stories are adapted from tales that appeared in a series of 12 girls' books published between 1895-1912 by L.C. Page and Co., now Doubleday and Co. Written by Annie Fellows Johnston, the girls' books were known as The Little Colonel series. A century later, they have been retold for today's young people.

The original "Waiting for True Love" appeared as "The Three Weavers" in *The Little Colonel at Boarding School.*

The original "In the Desert of Waiting" appeared in *The Little Colonel in Arizona.*

The original "Ederyn's Promise" appeared as "Keeping Tryst" in *The Little Colonel's Christmas Vacation.*

The original "The Enchanted Necklace" appeared in *The Little Colonel's House Party.*

The original "The Jester's Sword" appeared in *Mary Ware: The Little Colonel's Chum.*

The original "Princess Winsome and the Jade Dragon" appeared as "The Rescue of Princess Winsome" in *The Little Colonel's Hero.*

WAITING FOR TRUE LOVE

On the sixth day of January, commonly known as Twelfth Night, three daughters were born to three weavers in a village on the road to Camelot. Fields that normally bore crops of barley and rye lay barren and still under the winter snows that cloaked the village that January evening.

But in the village, all was merry as the fathers of the three girls celebrated the births of their firstborn. Their simple houses stood side by side, and whatever took place under the roof of one happened to all three. In appearance, the weavers wore the same gray tunics, wove the same patterns in their looms, sang the same songs, told the same tales and drank the same kind of broth from the same kind of bowls.

But their personalities were as unlike as could be. The merriest was Felix, who carelessly wove his mantles to any length that happened to be convenient, then stretched or cut it afterward to fit whoever would take it. He named his red-haired infant Felicity, after himself, and resolved that he would teach his daughter to enjoy life and take nothing seriously.

The saddest of the three was Christopher, who insisted on weaving all his mantles the same length, regardless of the size of the men who must wear them. He named his blonde-haired daughter Christina, after himself. Life was stern and hard for Christopher, and from the earliest days of her life, Christina sensed a brooding spirit about her father.

The third man was Sylvester, and he was neither overly happy or sad, but quiet and thoughtful. When he wove cloaks on his loom, with great painstaking care he measured first the man, then wove the mantle for a perfect fit. Life to him was sheer beauty. He resolved to teach his newborn daughter, Sylvia, that all things are possible to her who believes and does not give up. He named her Sylvia, not only after himself but after the nearby forests where dwelt wood nymphs that resembled his dark-haired daughter with her large brown eyes.

The day came when all three daughters were to be baptized. It was the Saturday before Easter, the day set aside for christenings. All the villagers gathered in their tiny stone church. The last child had just been sealed with the holy oil and the cross when a bright light filled the church. Floating above them was a being with flaming hair, white robes and a face so glorious and bright that few could look on it.

"I am Clotho," she said, "the guardian angel of all weavers. I have left beside the cradle of each child a tiny loom made of pure gold. For it is decreed in heaven that a royal prince shall seek to wed each child."

The villagers gasped with pleasure as well as envy toward the three weavers. Then the priest, a wise man of few words, spoke.

"What if they cannot fulfill all the conditions for a prince?" he asked. Clotho did not take offense at his question.

"One thing is necessary for such a marriage," the angel said. "Your daughters must weave upon each loom a royal mantle for the prince. It must be large and pleasant to look at, woven of golden thread of the quality and texture that would please a future king. Many will come to claim it, but if it is woven rightly, only the destined prince can wear it. It will fit him perfectly, like a falcon's feathers fit the falcon. But if it should not be ample and fine, ready for royal wearing, the prince will refuse to wear it and the maiden's heart shall break."

With a flash of stars, the angel disappeared.

The baptism remained the talk of the village for many months. No one doubted that these three special girls would each win their prince. One night the three weavers met to boast among themselves of the three kings' sons who should some day sit at their tables.

"I fear no trouble from this," said Christopher, after their dinner of wine and mincemeat pie," for I shall hide all knowledge of the magic loom from my daughter until she is full grown. Then I'll teach her how to weave this precious garment. Meanwhile, she shall learn all the things that a princess should know: Embroidery, needlework and how to play the harp. But her childish hands would make terrible work of the loom if I were to let her use the shuttle as she wished."

Felix shook his head. "Why bother yourself about such a trifle?" he exclaimed. "Why, no one could weave a mantle on such a tiny loom! It's but a toy that Clotho left the child to play with. She shall weave her dreams and fantasies on it however she wills. I will not interfere. What's decreed is decreed and nothing I can do will change it. And you, Sylvester?"

Sylvester said nothing but wondered if Clotho's conditions might not be a lot harder to keep than his friends supposed.

Months passed, the willows whitened, the trees turned golden, then tossed their leaves to carpet the willing earth. Winter came again but this time bearing the Angel of Death on its freezing winds. The Plague swept the country, wasting one third of the villagers, including the three mothers of the baby girls, for what happened under the roof of one weaver was bound to happen to all three. The villagers whispered that the three daughters miraculously survived due to Clotho's protection, for great destinies were in store for them.

Years passed and the maidens grew, playing together in the same garden and learning their daily lessons. They were as fond of each other as three sisters.

One day Felicity said to the others, "Come with me and I will show you a beautiful toy that Clotho left me at my baptism. My father says she gave one to each of us, and that it is decreed that we are each to wed a prince if we can weave for him a perfect mantle of gold cloth. Already I've begun to weave mine."

Silently, looking about for fear of watchful eyes and forbidding voices, the three girls tiptoed into an inner room at Felicity's house. She showed them her loom of gold. But it was no longer the tiny toy that had been left beside her cradle. For every inch she had grown, an inch had been added to the loom. The warp, which was the upright thread on the loom, was also Clotho's gift and it too grew with the maiden's growth. But the woof, the thread the shuttle carried, was the girl's own. It was the color of roses from the airy dreams of her girlish fantasies.

"See," Felicity whispered, "I have begun the mantle for my prince." Seizing the shuttle as she had seen her father do so many times, she crossed the golden warp with the woof thread of a rosy daydream. Christina and Sylvia looked on in silent envy, not so much for the loom as for the mirror that hung beside it. Most looms have mirrors that help the weaver see the other side of their tapestry. But this mirror was different; the angel had caused the mirror to show all the travelers on the road outside their village that led to Camelot.

"See?" said Felicity, pointing to the mirror, "look at that curly-haired shepherd lad! Doesn't he look like a prince as he strides by with his head held high and his blue eyes smiling upon all the world? He carries his shepherd's crook like a royal scepter. I am always at my mirror both at sunrise and sunset to watch him pass by with his sheep."

"That long-haired page with coal-black eyes in a red cloak is more to my liking," said Christina timidly. "He looks noble, as if he had been brought up in palaces. Why has my father never said a thing to me of Clotho's gift? I, too, should be at my weaving, for I am your age, Felicity."

"So am I," said Sylvia.

"Ask your fathers," Felicity said. "Maybe they forgot."

When Christina reached home, she went to her father Christopher and said, timidly, with her eyes fixed on the ground, "Father, where is my loom like Felicity's? I, too, would be weaving for my prince."

But Christopher glowered and shook with anger. "Who told you of what has been decreed?" He spoke so sternly that she trembled in fear. "You must not listen to such false stories! When you are a grown woman, you may come to me and I will talk to you then of weaving and looms, but why are you asking me of such things now? You silly child! I am ashamed that a daughter of mine should think such foolish things!"

Christina crept away to weep in shame for having provoked her father. But the next day, as they were playing in the garden, Felicity said, "Your father is an old tyrant to forbid you to use Clotho's gift. He cannot love you as my father loves me or he would not deny you such a pleasure. Come! Let's go look for it."

Christina hesitated, feeling unsure at the thought of going against her father's wishes, even though they seemed unjust. But surely there was no harm in looking at this beautiful gift. So hand in hand they searched out a hidden room with a door that Christina thought was securely bolted. It was unlocked and inside the tiny room stood a loom like Felicity's and over it a mirror in which the same images of the world were played out. Christina picked up the shuttle to send the thread of her rosy daydream through the warp of gold. The long-haired page in the red cloak walked down the road to Camelot that moment and she saw him in the mirror.

"How like a prince he carries himself!" she murmured. "My father is indeed a tyrant to deny me the pleasure of looking out upon the world and weaving sweet fancies about it. Therefore I will not obey him but will sneak away each day in here, to weave in secret what he will not allow me to do openly."

At the same time, Sylvia stood before her father, shyly saying, "Is it true what Felicity says has been decreed in heaven for me? Today, after I saw her loom, I pushed back the bolt that has always barred the door leading into the inner room from mine, and there I found the loom of gold and a magical mirror. I would like to use them as Felicity does, but I wanted to ask your permission first."

A very tender smile lit up the face of her father as he gazed down at the serious brown eyes fixed on him. Taking her little hand in his, he led the way into the inner room. "I have often looked forward to this day, my little one," he exclaimed, "although I did not think you would come so soon with your questions. What Felicity has told you is indeed true and has been decreed for you. However, your future happiness—and that of your children—depends on how you weave this mantle.

"Felicity's father did not tell her that," Sylvia said.

"He would have done well to remember all of what was said at your baptism," Sylvester responded. "It is a dangerous gift the good Clotho left you, for the higher you aim, the lower you may fall. When you look in that mirror, you will be tempted to weave your mantle to fit whatever men appear therein. Only listen to your father who has never yet deceived you and who has only your good at heart."

He left the room and came back with something Sylvia had never seen before: a gleaming silver yardstick.

"Always keep this by your side," he said. "It is no ordinary yardstick. It marks the feet and the inches to which the height of a prince must measure. Not until the mantle is fully equal to that height can it be safely taken from the loom.

"You are so young, and it is at best a little mantle you could weave this year. It would clothe the shoulders of the shepherd lad but no one else," he said, pointing to the shepherd's reflection in the mirror. "But it is a blessed loom that lengthens with your growth and each year the mantle will grow longer, until as a grown woman, you can hold it up against the yardstick and find that it measures exactly to the inch the size demanded by the prince's noble height. For a prince will demand all the gold thread you have in your possession; you cannot afford to waste one inch of it on another man.

"But you will often be dazzled by the mirror's sights, and youths will come to you, one by one, each begging, `Give *me* the royal mantle, Sylvia! I am the prince destined for you.' And with honeyed words he'll show you how the mantle in the loom is just the right length to fit *his* shoulders. But don't let him persuade you to cut it loose and give it to him, as you will want to do.

"Weave on another year and yet another, until you, a grown woman, can measure out a perfect mantle. This mantle will be larger and more grand than ever those youths could carry, but it will fit your prince faultlessly, like the falcon's feathers fit the falcon."

Sylvia was awed by his solemn words. She took the silver yardstick and hung it by the mirror. Standing before her father, she said, "You may trust me, father. I will not cut the golden warp from the loom until I, a grown woman, have woven such a mantle as you yourself will say is worthy of a prince."

Sylvester placed his hands on her head, prayed a blessing over her and a prayer for wisdom, then returned to his work. After that, the winter followed the autumn and the summer followed the spring many times, and the children played in the garden and learned embroidery, needlework and how to play the harp. Each day, each girl went to her inner room and threw the shuttle in and out among the threads of gold.

Christina always worked in secret, peering into the mirror, afraid the long-haired page in the red cloak would slip by and she not see him. The color of his jet-black hair dazzled her to all other sights and his face was all she thought of by day and dreamed of by night, so that she often forgot to thread her needle or practice her music. He was only a page, but she called him prince in her thoughts until she really believed him one. When she worked at the loom, she sang to herself, "It is for him, for him!"

Felicity laughed openly about her weaving and her father often teased her about the one for whom her mantle was intended. Whenever the village lads went by, her father would say, "Is that your prince?" or "Are you weaving for this one?" But he never went with her into that inner room, so he never knew whether the weaving was done well or poorly. He never knew that she cut the web of one year's weaving and gave it to the curly-haired shepherd. He wore it with jaunty grace at first, and Felicity spent long hours at the mirror, watching to see him pass by all wrapped within its folds. But it grew grimy with use, especially with his long tramps over the dirty moors after his flocks. Felicity saw other figures in her mirror who pleased her better and she began another mantle.

She gave that mantle to a student and the next she gave to a troubadour strolling past her window and the next to a knight in armor who rode by one idle summer day. Once she saw a prince in her mirror at a great distance and the memory of who the mantle was destined for overwhelmed her. But then a handsome squire came into the village square and she forgot her serious thoughts.

As Felicity scattered her favors, Christina labored on, faithful to the page alone. Sylvia likewise worked on, true to her promise. But there came a time when a face shone across her mirror so noble and fair that she gasped.

"O, surely it's him," she whispered to her father. "His eyes are so blue they fill all my dreams."

But Sylvester answered, "Does he measure up to the standard set by the silver yardstick for a full-grown prince?"

"No," she answered sadly. "Only to the measure of an ordinary man. But see how perfectly the mantle I have woven would fit him!"

"No, weave on," he said kindly. "You have not done your best. This is not the man decreed for you."

A few months later, a knight's face flashed across her mirror; a knight like Sir Lancelot of King Arthur's round table. He was headed toward Camelot and he looked so noble that she felt sure that he was the one destined to wear her mantle. She went to her father, saying insistently, "He has asked for the mantle, and measured by your own silver yardstick, it would almost fit him perfectly."

Sylvester laid the yardstick against the mantle. "No," he said. "This is only the size of a knight. It lacks yet an inch of the measure of a prince."

Sylvia hesitated, half pouting, until he said, beseechingly, "I am an old man now. I know far more of the world and its ways than do you, my daughter. Have I ever deceived you? Have I ever had anything but your good at heart? Have a little more patience. Wait another year and you will be able to weave a still larger mantle."

That was the last lengthy conversation they had with each other. The next day, villagers came running to Sylvia to tell her that her father had been kicked in the head by a horse while harnessing it to a cart. He never regained consciousness and died one cold morning a few days later. Standing by his grave, Sylvia realized that now there was no one to help her choose her prince. The next time someone rode by, she would be on her own.

But no one came and Sylvia took over her father's business, weaving day and night. Although she was barely an inch away from the perfect mantle, she had no time to work on it except between midnight and dawn, when her hands were too heavy with sleep and too cold to obey her.

The following April, a prince came riding by to ask for Christina as his bride. Christopher took her by the hand and said, "Now I will lead you into the inner room and teach you how to use the angel's sacred gift. With me for a teacher, you will surely make no mistake."

When they came to the inner room, there stood only the empty loom from which the golden warp had been clipped.

"What happened?" he demanded angrily. Christina, braving his bad humor as she had for years, said defiantly, "You are too late. Because I feared your scorn of what you called my childish 'foolishness,' I wove the mantle in secret, and when my prince came by a few months ago, I gave it to him. He's standing outside now."

Turning in rage, the astonished father saw the long-haired page cloaked in the mantle that she had woven. He tore it angrily from the youth and demanded she give it to the prince. But the prince would have none of it, for it had been defiled from being worn by a common page. After one look of disdain, he rode away.

Stripped of the robe her own fancy had woven around him, the page stood shorn before her. She no longer saw him as her fond dreams had painted him but in all his unworthiness. The mantle lay in tattered shreds at her feet. When she looked from one to the other and saw the mistake she had made and the opportunity she had lost, she covered her face with her hands and cried out to Christopher, "It is *your* fault! You shouldn't have laughed in scorn at my childish questions, thus driving me to weave in ignorance and in secret!" But all her blaming was too late. For her heart broke, as Clotho warned it might, and she fled to a convent in the next village where she remained for the rest of her life.

That same month, Sylvia's shipment of woven goods were stolen on the way to the market and she had no money left to buy fine wool. She went to the village priest who had baptized her and who, now that her father was gone, she trusted more than anyone else.

"What shall I do?" she asked. Remembering the baby girl he had held 18 years before, the priest noticed how forlorn and lonely and tired she looked.

"What is most precious to you?" he asked.

Knowing what had happened to Christina, Sylvia realized that the mantle on her loom was her most precious possession, for it was the key to a royal destiny. Yet in all these years, no prince had come.

"The loom I was given at birth," she said, sadly.

"Sell the rest of what you have," the priest told her, "to buy yourself time to finish the mantle."

Sylvia wept but sold the last of the woven goods her father had left her, receiving enough money to last two more months.

That May, a prince came to Felix, asking for his daughter. He called her from the garden, saying gaily, "Bring forth the mantle now, Felicity. Surely it must be a good one after all these years of weaving."

She brought it forth but when Felix saw it, he was aghast at its tiny size. When he demanded the reason, she confessed she had no more of the golden warp that Clotho had given her. She had squandered her maiden love in past years to make mantles for the shepherd, the troubadour, the student and the knight. This was all she had left to give.

"Well," said her father at length, "it's only what many another has done in the foolishness of youth. But perhaps when the prince sees how fair you are and how sweetly you sing and play the harp, he may overlook the paltriness of your offering. Take it to him."

When she had laid the mantle before him, the prince cast only one glance at it because it was so small, so meager of gold thread and so unfit for a true prince's wearing. He looked sorrowfully into the depths of her beautiful green eyes and turned away.

That gaze burned into her very soul and revealed to her all she had lost for evermore. She cried out to her father with sobs that cut into his heart. "It is *your* fault!" she said. "Why didn't you warn me what a precious gift Clotho's golden thread was? Why did you say to me, `Is this the lad? Is that the lad?' until I looked only at the unworthy men of the village and forgot how high is the height of a perfect prince?" Then, like Christina, her heart broke and Felicity fled from the village toward the coast where it was said she found a ship ready to set sail. She boarded it and was never seen again.

On the first of June, Sylvia ran out of Clotho's golden thread. That very evening, as the sunset lit the sky with flaming clouds, her prince arrived, surrounded by a vast retinue of courtiers, heralds and swordsmen in glittering mail shirts. Bearing torches, they accompanied the prince to the weavers' cottages, where he alighted from his white stallion and knocked on Sylvia's door. The villagers came to gawk at this king's son with a silver bugle by his side and a red cross on his shield. He carried himself so nobly that they whispered that here was someone equal to King Arthur himself.

Trembling, Sylvia clipped the threads that held the gold and rose mantle and let the prince take it from her. Glancing shyly up, she saw it fit him perfectly, as the falcon's feathers fit the falcon. The crowd cheered with a shout that filled the valley and caused the evening stars to blaze in the purple twilight.

Their wedding was on Midsummer Night's Eve in a gold and white pavilion on a flowery field. The moment the priest pronounced his blessing on the couple, there was a blaze of light and Clotho appeared before the crowd. The angel stretched out her hands in blessing.

"Because even as a child you did as your father told you to do, because you were wise and didn't squander a single strand of the golden thread on another, because you were patient and waited until your woman's fingers wove the best that lay within your woman's heart, all happiness shall be yours!" she proclaimed. "Receive it as your perfect crown!"

With the angelic blessing upon her, Sylvia rode away beside the prince to Camelot, her life was crowned with happiness as it had been decreed for her in heaven.

IN THE DESERT OF WAITING

Far off in the deserts of Arabia lived a young Arab named Shapur. He was brought up in barren wastes of blazing white sand by day and luminous stars by night. His parents had died during a famine when he was young but miraculously, he had survived to be raised by his cousins. They were a band of fierce desert warriors who loved war and spent long summer evenings creating poems and ballads about the heroic exploits of their tribe.

But Shapur was a peaceful young man with a gracious manner, handsome looks and no taste nor talent for a life of desert warfare. Instead, he longed to explore the fabled metropolises to the west of their domain: Cities with high towers and minarets that overlooked vast hanging gardens of orange, lemon and sandalwood trees surrounding pools with tiled bottoms and splashing fountains.

On the day he turned 20, he entered the tent of Aziz, the eldest of his relatives.

"O most honored cousin," he began.

"By the holy books, what is it you want?" asked Aziz, fingering his jeweled dagger.

"Our law provides that the nearest of kin take care of orphans and so you have done, most honored Aziz," Shapur replied. "I could not thank you for a thousand years for your generosity. May He who rules from the heavens reward you."

Aziz cocked his eyebrows and remained silent.

"I have come to ask you a favor," Shapur continued.

"Is it a wife you wish?" Aziz asked. "It is high time you began raising sons to succeed you."

Shapur sighed. His cousin never could think much beyond a day's

21

journey of his tents. "No, most fortunate cousin," he replied. "Before I take a bride, I must prove my manhood, if to no one else but myself. Grant me leave to earn an honorable profit by selling some precious commodity in the City of Desire."

Aziz whistled. "You have high hopes, cousin," he replied. Both men had heard of the fabled City of Desire that lay far away across the sands. Of its eight gates, the most famous was the Golden Gate, opened only one day a year to admit visiting princes from distant cities. Any who were so fortunate to fall in with these royal retinues would follow them to the king's palace and to its courtyard. Wares displayed there for sale brought fabulous sums, a hundred times greater than when sold in the open market.

Only to a privileged few would the Golden Gate open at any other time. It would turn on its hinges for anyone sent at a king's request, or anyone bearing an extremely rare gift. But no common sheik, such as Shapur, could ever wish to pass its shining portal, except on this one day.

Aziz shrugged, then motioned to a tent across the way.

"Therein lies the treasure of our tribe," he said. "Many from other tribes come to us to buy the salt that we have stored up here. You may take a load of it to sell in the City of Desire. But that is all you shall receive from me. Do not return to this spot again penniless. Only if you make your fortune shall you be welcome in our tents."

Shapur bowed and tried to hide his pleasure. He was glad to leave his cousins and a load of salt would easily earn him a living anywhere he would go. It was extremely marketable; not only was it a token of hospitality, but salt was needed to preserve meat. He cleared his throat.

"Most generous cousin, I am deeply honored," he said. "In order for me to depart, I beg once more to draw from the well of your generosity in one more matter . . ." his voice trailed off and Aziz followed Shapur's glance to the herd of camels grazing by the tents.

"Of course, cousin," Aziz said. "Did you think I would neglect your transport?"

On the day of Shapur's departure, his cousins led up a leggy, young camel to his side and Shapur's heart sank. Why, this was barely an adult, he thought. The camel was like him: Young and untested. He gripped the bags of salt he had packed and began loading them on the one-humped beast who proved equal to the heavy load. Shapur noticed that his new companion seemed good-humored, since most camels will just as soon spit as look at you and are rarely in a good mood. His name, Shapur learned, was Kalam, meanng 'speech' in their tongue. Shapur climbed atop Kalam, waved at the only family he had had for many years, then rode off.

It was a wealthy caravan, laden with merchandise for far distant markets and flanked by Persian soldiers brought along to guard the merchants from bandits. Some of the camels bore in their packs wineskins of the richest vintage of the Orient. Other camels bore tapestries, carpets, expensive weavings and spices such as cinnamon, rosemary, frankincense and myrrh or perfumes made from essences of jasmine, lavender, rosewood or violets. Still more camels were loaded with gold, baskets containing cobras, rare purple dye, jeweled boxes of topaz, rubies and pearls. Shapur rode in front of the caravan, urging Kalam on with haste. In his heart burned the desire to be first to enter the Golden Gate to display his wares.

A week later, they came upon an oasis where they rested and enjoyed fresh waters from its sparkling fountains. The next morning, when the merchants were reloading their camels, Shapur's camel stumbled into a hidden hole and sank upon the sand in pain.

In vain he urged it to continue its journey but the poor lame beast could not rise under its great load.

Sack by sack he lessened its burden, throwing each off grudgingly and with great sighs, for he did not want to lose any of his prospective fortune. But, even rid of its entire load, the camel could not rise. The other merchants urged Shapur to leave Kalam at the oasis so that at least he would reach the City of Desire. But Shapur had no wish to enter the city penniless with no salt at all and he had grown fond of his good-natured camel. His companions left without him.

For many days and nights he watched beside Kalam, bringing him water from the fountain and feeding him with the lush green plants by the oasis. At last he was rewarded by seeing the camel struggle to its feet and take a few limping steps. But in his distress at being left behind by the caravan, Shapur had not noticed where he had thrown the load of salt. A tiny stream, trickling from the fountain, had run through the sacks and dissolved the precious mineral. When he went to gather up his load, only a single sackful was left.

"Now the Almighty has indeed forgotten me!" he cried. Cursing the day he was born, he tore off his white headdress and beat upon his breast. Even if his camel was able to set out across the desert, it would be useless to seek a market now that he had no merchandise. He sat on the ground, his head bowed in his hands, consumed by despair.

When he looked again at his poor camel standing unsteadily near the palm trees, he cried out, "Ah, woe is me! Of all created things, I am the most miserable! Of all dooms, mine is the most unjust! Why should I, with life beating strong in my veins and ambition like a fire in my breast, be left here helpless on the sands? Here I can achieve nothing and can make no progress toward the City of Desire."

One day, as he sat thus under the cool date palms, a bee buzzed about him. He brushed it away, but it returned so persistently that he looked up.

"Where there are bees, there must be honey," he said. "If there be any sweetness in this desert, better that I should go in its quest than sit here bewailing my fate."

Leaving the camel grazing by the fountain, he followed the bee. For many miles he pursued it, until far in the distance he beheld the palm trees of another oasis. He quickened his steps, for an odor rare as the perfumes of paradise floated out to meet him. The bee had led him to the rose garden of Omar.

Now Omar was an alchemist, a wise man with the power to transform the most common earthly elements into precious metals. Popular lore had it that he was rich beyond belief, with the ability to transform the basest of objects into pure gold. The fame of his skill had spread to far countries, even to the fabled land of Spain west of the great sea. So many pilgrims sought his expert touch that the question, "Where is the house of Omar?" was heard daily even in the City of Desire. Shapur had heard talk of it among the merchants of his caravan.

But for a generation, that question had remained unanswered. And now here it was before him: A fabulously rich dwelling of cut marble, cooled by springs that flowed underneath. Only he and the bees knew where he was; they because of the vast rose gardens surrounding Omar's home. Following the bee, Shapur found himself in the old man's presence.

After Omar invited him into his cool home to rest, sip cold mint tea and dine on yogurt and cucumbers, Shapur told his story.

Now Omar was as wise as he was rich and he could discern the minds of men as readily as unrolled parchments. Sensing Shapur's innocence and gentleness, he was touched by his misfortune.

He finally said, "You may think that because I am Omar, with the power to transform all common things into precious things, that I could easily take the remnant of salt still left to you in your sack and change it into gold. Then you could joyfully go on to the City of Desire as soon as your camel is able to carry you, far richer for your delay."

Shapur's heart gave a bound of hope, for this is truly what he had been thinking. But his heart sank at Omar's next words.

"No, Shapur, each man must carry out his own destiny. Believe me, for you the desert holds a greater opportunity than kings' houses could offer. Give me your patient service in this time of waiting and I will share such secrets with you that, when you finally arrive at the Golden Gate, it shall be with precious wares and a kingly character to gain for you a royal entrance.

Thinking deeply, Shapur walked the long miles underneath the hot afternoon sky back to his camel. As the moon rose, he urged it to its feet and led it slowly across the sands. Because it could still bear no burden, he lifted the remaining sack of salt to his own back. The moon was shining brightly overhead, making the rose garden glisten with pearly light, when Shapur arrived back at Omar's gates.

He knocked, calling, "Here am I, Omar, at your bidding, and here is the remnant of my salt. All that I have left I offer you and stand ready to give my patient service."

Then Omar had him lead his camel to a fountain where he could feed on the leafy plants surrounding its cool waters. Pointing to a row of great stone jars, he said, "There is your work. Every morning before sunrise, they must be filled with rose petals plucked from the thousands of roses in my garden. Then, fill the jars with water from the fountain."

"A task for poets," thought Shapur as he began. "What could be more delightful than to stand in the moonlit garden and pluck the velvet leaves?" But after awhile the thorns tore his hands and the rustle and hiss underfoot revealed the presence of snakes. Sleep weighed heavily on Shapur's eyelids. It was monotonous work, standing hour after hour stripping rose leaves until thousands and thousands and thousands had been dropped into the great jars. The very sweetness of the task began to wear upon him.

When the stars grew pale and the east was brightening, old Omar came out. "Well done," he said. "Now have breakfast and sleep today to prepare for another night."

Another busy night passed, and another until weeks went by. It seemed to Shapur that he had picked the garden 10 times over. But for every rose he plucked, two bloomed in its place, and night after night he filled the jars. He learned to carry a lantern with him to ward off the snakes. To stay awake, he repeated to himself Arabic poetry he had learned as a youth.

Still, he was learning no secrets and he asked himself questions. Wasn't he wasting his life? Wouldn't it have been better to have waited by the oasis until another caravan passed by that would carry him out of the solitude to the dwellings of men? What opportunity could the desert offer?

The thorns continued to make his hands bleed. The lonely silence of the starry desert nights weighed on him. He would have left his task many times, but for the shadowy form of his sand-colored camel kneeling by the fountain. One night he would have sworn Kalam spoke to him. It had sounded like a whisper through the starlight, "Patience, Shapur, have patience!"

Once, far in the distance at dawn, he saw the black outline of a caravan passing along the horizon. Gazing after it with a fierce longing to follow, he pictured the scenes it was moving toward: Gilded minarets, rich palaces, the cries of the populace and all the life and stir of the marketplace. When the distant procession had passed, the great silence of the desert hit him with a deeper pain.

He thought of giving up, but again he saw his faithful camel, who seemed to whisper, "Patience, Shapur, have patience! Someday you too shall travel to the City of Desire."

Hope rose up in his heart. Maybe the All-Knowing One had not forgotten him. For some reason, heaven had ordained that he should be here, picking these endless rose petals. Maybe there was a purpose to this long delay

Months went by until one day in the waning of summer, Omar called him into a room Shapur had never seen before.

"Now at last," Omar said, "you have proven yourself worthy to share my secrets. Come! I will show you. Thus are the roses distilled and thus is gathered up the precious oil floating at the mouths of these jars.

"Do you see this tiny bottle? It weighs but an ounce, but it took the sweetness of 200,000 roses to make the perfume it contains and it is so costly that only princes can afford it. It is worth far more than your entire load of salt that was washed away at the fountain."

Shapur gasped at the sight of the crystal bottle, sealed with a red wax seal and filled with the precious perfume. Omar placed it in Shapur's rough and worn hands.

"You have done well, Shapur!" Omar said. "Behold the gift of the desert, its reward for your patient service. Wherever you go, its sweetness will open for you a way and win for you a welcome. You came into the desert a vendor of salt. You will go forth a changed man, found worthy to bear this royal perfume after your long wait.

"Wherever," Omar continued, "you see a heart bowed down in some Desert of Waiting, you will whisper to it, 'Patience! Here, if you will, in these arid lands, you will find your Garden of Omar, and from these daily tasks that prick you so sorely, you will distill the precious perfume of sympathy to sweeten all life. But it is only gotten at great cost. And no one fills their crystal vase with it until they have been pricked by the world's disappointments and bowed by its tasks.

"So like the bee that led you to my teaching, so shall you lead others to hope."

With a shock, Shapur realized that the test of manhood that he had long sought was complete. Prostrating himself before Omar, he then joyfully placed the crystal vase in the inside pocket of his robe, then went in search of Kalam. Totally healed after the long months of waiting, Kalam bore him swiftly across the sands to the City of Desire. The Golden Gate,which would not have opened to the vendor of salt, swung wide for Shapur, his camel and their precious merchandise.

Princes brought their pearls to exchange for his perfume and even Aziz and his family heard of Shapur's fame and came to pay their respects to him. Everywhere he went, the sweetness of the perfume won for him a royal welcome. Wherever he saw a heart bowed down in some Desert of Waiting, he whispered Omar's words.

Years later, at his death, in order that no one forget, he asked that his tomb be placed at the oasis where he and his camel had been delayed. There, in the midst of the arid desert, he caused to be cut in stone that emblem of patience: The camel, kneeling on the sand. It bore this inscription that all could see, as they toiled toward their City of Desire:

"Patience! Here, if you will, on these arid sands, you may find your Garden of Omar. Even from the daily tasks that prick you sorely, you may distill precious perfume to greatly bless you and all those you will meet. Then shall you arrive at your City of Desire."

EDERYN'S PROMISE

One cold night just before Christmas, a troubadour stopped by the gates of a castle on rolling hills in England's southern reaches. Further to the south lay the sea and south of that were the lands of oranges and palm branches and olive trees where winter never came, of which troubadours loved to sing.

The folk in the castle invited the troubadour in and asked him to play his harp for the lords and ladies who were gathered for amusement after supper. After helping himself to soup and bread, the troubadour seated himself by the roaring fire and came face to face with a child about seven years old. The troubadour guessed from his pale skin and blond hair that the boy was an orphan brought back from some Saxon raid to the icy countries to the north. With some reluctance, the child admitted his name was Ederyn, a humble page assigned to serve one of the many squires residing in the household of the great earl.

"Do my songs please you?" the troubadour asked playfully, smiling at the upturned face.

"O sir," the youth responded, "on such a winged song, the soul could fly to heaven! But tell me, is it possible for one such as I to be like one of the knights of whom you sing?"

The troubadour gazed for a little while into the Yule log's flame, then stroked his long gray beard. "Some lads like you become knights and win royal acclaim because the blood of dragons stains their hands," he finally replied. "The king rewards them mightily for such victorious combat. And some are scarred by defeating the giants that prey upon the borders of our fair domain. Some have traveled on crusades to faraway lands and there have proved their faithfulness to the king."

Ederyn sighed, for he well knew that his thin body could never fight a dragon nor were his arms strong enough to wrestle with giants. Being bound to the squire, he could never get permission to seek adventures in faraway places.

"Is there no other way?" he asked.

"I think not," the troubadour replied. "But take an old man's counsel. Forget your dreams of glory and be content to serve your squire. For what have you to do with such great ambitions?" The child crept away sadly.

The year passed and once again it was Christmas. The troubadour arrived at the great hall in the falling snow and made his listeners merry with his songs of Camelot. He sang of knights and fair ladies, of love and death and valor. Ederyn again crept close to listen. Remembering the impossibility of rising above his humble station in life, he sighed and hung his head.

The troubadour noticed Ederyn and remembered his question of the year before. "Well, now, sad one," he whispered to Ederyn, "I bring you tidings that should make you sing for joy. There is a way for you to become a knight. I heard it at the royal court before Arthur's very throne."

Ederyn eagerly leaned closer.

"Know this," the troubadour explained. "It is the king's desire to establish around him at his court in Camelot a circle of faithful people whose fidelity has stood the highest tests. No deeds of strength are required of these true followers nor any great conquests. However, they must prove themselves trustworthy so it may be said of them, 'In all things faithful.'

"Only those who are faithful concerning small things will be entrusted with great things. The king has given to Merlin the enchanter the task of finding those who are faithful.

"Now listen!" the troubadour continued. "Each day at daybreak, the king, through the wizard Merlin, will send an enchanted call throughout the kingdom for those who have ears to hear. They must wake at dawn to listen in high places for only then are the voices of the world still enough for the call to be heard. The time of testing will be long, the summons many. You will be called to duty and to sorrow, to disappointment and to defeat but no matter what the call, there is but one reply if you would be a knight. Listen and I will teach you how to answer this call."

Strumming his harp, the troubadour sang softly:

> "It's the king's call! I must
> Obey this destiny so high
> No matter the pain, stay true,
> Be faithful, or die!"

Then Ederyn, his hand upon his heart, made a solemn promise.

"I will await that call daily, awaking at dawn and listening in high places. I will follow where it leads. Even if the path lies through fire or flood, I'll have this one reply:

> "It's the king's call! I must
> Obey this destiny so high
> No matter the pain, stay true,
> Be faithful, or die!"

That night, Ederyn climbed up the steps of a tower next to the hall and faced the east. Below in the banquet hall, the festivities became louder and more drunken, but Ederyn remained at his post.

As gray dawn trailed across the hills, he jumped to his feet. Far away sounded the call for which he had been waiting. It was like the faint blowing of an elfin horn, but the words were clear.

"Ederyn! Ederyn! One awaits you tonight in the shade of the yew tree by the abbey tower! Keep your promise!"

Ederyn did not need to reply. He only had to obey. Now the abbey tower was five miles from the domain of the earl and Ederyn knew quite well that only by special permission of his squire would he be allowed to make this journey. From sunrise to sunset, he worked hard to gain the desired leave. Never had the squire's buckles shone so brightly as when Ederyn polished them that day. Even the most menial tasks ceased to be so humbling once Ederyn set to work on them. By dusk, he had performed all his duties so well that the squire allowed him to go.

The way was long and when Ederyn reached the tree by the abbey tower, he trembled in fear upon seeing a ghostly spirit standing beneath the tree. It had no face, nor did it hold anything in its hands. His knees knocking, Ederyn approached it, saying, "I am Ederyn, come to obey the king's call."

The specter replied, "Well have you kept it, for it is known to me the many menial tasks you performed before you could leave on your quest. As a symbol of our meeting, here is my pledge that you may show the king."

Ederyn felt a light touch on the inside of his shirt and suddenly he found himself alone beside the shadowy abbey. His hands clammy with fear, he drew his cloak about him and raced home as if in the middle of a nightmare. Arriving just before daybreak, he almost believed it had all been a dream. But, when he removed his vest and cloak, he saw a pearl gleaming on his shirt where the spirit's hand had touched him. It was a token to the king that he had answered faithfully to his call.

As dawn lit the sky, he climbed the tower stairs and listened for the summons. Again, it was clear and sweet, like a distant horn of the elves. It cried, "Ederyn! Ederyn! One awaits you at midnight beside black Kilgore's water. Keep your promise!"

That day, he worked extra hard to gain his squire's permission to travel away from the hall. This time, his task was counting all the spears and iron pikes. He also counted the shorter battle axes and coats of mail that filled the earl's storehouse. Over and over he counted until his eyes ached. At last his task was done and the squire praised him for his work. Once again Ederyn was permitted to take his nighttime journey.

After a few hours of sleep, he undertook the dreadful trek to the waters of Kilgore. By midnight he was at the right spot, where another ghostly spirit awaited him. It, too, left a touch upon his shirt in token that he had been faithful. When he looked, another pearl gleamed there beside the first.

Many days passed and Ederyn never failed in his humble tasks. Instead, he did his ordinary duties as if they were mighty battle deeds. With his squire's permission, he gained the freedom to meet with every messenger Merlin sent.

Once he traveled along a dangerous road that crossed a gruesome swamp filled with green slime and creeping things. He wanted to flee, but for the sake of his promise, he crossed the swamp and reached his goal. When he looked inside his cloak to see what token he had earned, a shining golden star lay over his heart above the rows of white pearls.

Ten years passed and Ederyn grew both in height and moral stature. One day, his squire was killed by robbers and Ederyn, in reward for his faithfulness, was made a squire in the man's place. Soon afterwards, the earl took Ederyn for a journey to a great lord who lived in the Castle of Content. The castle had a beautiful garden and the new squire had all the free time he wished. No dreary tasks were given him there. He could wander down miles of garden paths, gaze at the fountain in the courtyard or watch the maidens at their tasks. And there was one among them, with a face like a lily and a gentle voice, with whom Ederyn fell in love. His promise grew dim in his memory and he was glad when, for a time, the king's call ceased in the mornings. He rejoiced even more when it came time for the earl to leave and it was decided that Ederyn would remain behind at the Castle of Content.

Still, Ederyn remained faithful to his vow to climb to a high place every dawn, when the voices of the world were still, to listen for Merlin's horn. One morning it came.

"Ederyn! Ederyn! One waits for you far away. By the black cave of Atropos, by the light of the full moon, keep your promise!

It was a full seven-day journey to the cave and Ederyn, thinking of the lily maid, was reluctant to leave the garden. He lingered by the fountain until late that night, saying to himself, "Why should I continue on longer in these foolish quests, meeting with shadows that vanish at my touch? I'm hardly nearer to being a knight than, when as a young page, I listened to the troubadour."

The fountain softly splashed and the sound of music floated from within the banquet hall. As Ederyn listened to the lily maiden sing, he forgot his promise. But a star reflected in the fountain waters made him look up into the bejeweled sky, where the morning star would appear in a few hours. With remorse, he remembered his early morning task of listening to Merlin's call. He rushed out of the garden into the night, clanging the castle's great gate behind him.

Strange and fearful woods lay between him and the cave; the wind moaned and even the trees seemed afraid. Nameless fears clutched at his heart, chilling his bones. Shadows seemed to pursue him. Suddenly, the earth caved in beneath his feet and black water closed in over his head. He had fallen in the pool that lies at the far edge of the fearful woods, a whirlpool so deep that only by the fiercest struggle could he escape. He was so cold that he considered allowing himself to drown, but the troubadour's song echoed in his heart:

> "It's the king's call. I must
> Obey this destiny so high
> No matter the pain, stay true,
> Be faithful, or die!"

With that, he dragged himself to land. He saw the cave a few yards away and by sheer force of will he crept to it, then fainted.

When he revived, a pale, full yellow moon was high in the sky. A form cloaked in black bowed over him.

"Ederyn," she sighed. "Here is your token that the king may know that you have met me face to face."

He gazed on his shirt and thought at first a diamond had landed there. But no, nothing but a tear drop glistened by the star. Sore and tired, he dragged himself back to the Castle of Content.

After that, the summons came often. Whenever all the world seemed loveliest and life most sweet, then was the call most sure to come. But he never faltered. He was never faithless to the king's command. As more years passed, he climbed mountains to find the somber face of Disaster waiting for him. Suffering and Pain were often at the end of his journey and once he met Defeat. But he bravely learned to smile into their eyes, no matter which one handed him the pledge of duty performed.

One day when he was a full-grown man, he heard the call he had dreamed of for fifteen years: "Ederyn! Ederyn! The king himself commands you to come and meet him the morning of Midsummer's Eve beside the palace gate."

His reward in sight, Ederyn sped toward Camelot. He arrived before the palace gate three days before the appointed time. But there came prowling through the woods a troop of dwarves along with the giant Shudderwain. Anxious to serve the cruel giant, the dwarves attacked Ederyn while he slept, bound him and dragged him into a nearby dungeon.

For two days, Ederyn lay trapped in the dungeon, raging over how he had been deprived of his reward at the last moment. Like a madman, he chewed on the ropes that bound him and threw himself against the stone walls of his prison. Eventually he freed himself from the ropes but to no avail. The wall of his prison was too high for him to vault over. From time to time, the dwarves peered at him from above and made fun of him.

"Don't count on keeping your promise," they called out. "But if you will return to the joyous garden and listen no more to Merlin's call, we'll free you from this Dungeon of Disappointment."

Ederyn was quite tempted, for the dungeon stank and he desired the lily maiden. But he plugged his ears with his fingers and cried out,

> "It's the king's call. I must
> Obey this destiny so high
> No matter the pain, stay true
> Be faithful, or die."

The night before Midsummer's Eve, he lay on the floor of the dungeon, exhausted. A moonbeam shone through the window above him. By its light, he saw a spider spinning a web. Looking around, he saw the dungeon was hung thick with many webs. As the spider swung itself back and forth, Ederyn's hopeless gaze followed it.

Suddenly, he realized what the spider was teaching him. He rushed against the dungeon walls and tore down all the dusty webs, twisting them in long strands, braiding these strands into thick ropes, tying them, knotting them, twisting and doubling again.

While doing so, he berated himself for wasting so much time.

"Three days ago I might have left this dungeon," he sighed, "had I but used the means that lay at hand. I now know that heaven always finds a way to help. No creature lives that cannot serve and even dungeon walls can help him who boldly grasps the first thing he sees and makes it serve him."

Before long, he had made the cobweb rope strong enough to bear his weight. After many trials, he succeeded in tossing the rope over a spike that barred the window. Climbing up and out, he then tied the rope's end to the window and slid down the cliffside into which the dwarves had dug the dungeon.

But by then it was dawn, the morning of Midsummer's Eve, the longest day of the year. Running through the woods, he reached the palace gate just as it opened for the king to ride forth. When Ederyn saw the royal procession, he shrunk back into the bushes, not wanting to appear before the king covered with the dungeon's filth.

But he knew he had to show that he had been faithful. As the king approached, he strode out of the woods and knelt, throwing aside his cloak. All the pledges he had faithfully kept throughout the years suddenly appeared on his shirt, glistening in the sunlight. There Pain had dropped her heart's blood in a glittering ruby and Honor had set her seal upon him in a golden star. A diamond gleamed where Sorrow's tear had fallen and amethysts glowed with purple splendor to mark his patient meeting with Defeat.

But most impressive were the pledges of little pearls for little duties faithfully performed. As the king's retinue gazed, they saw the jewels take the shape of letters, forming four words: "In all things faithful."

King Arthur drew his royal sword Excalibur and lightly touched Ederyn's shoulder, knighting him.

"Arise, Sir Ederyn the Faithful," the king cried. "Now I may trust you to the utmost in little things as well as great. Since you have been faithful in lesser things, you shall be given greater tasks. From now on, ride by my side to be my faithful guard and friend."

The king ordered that a horse be brought for Ederyn, a sword buckled on him and golden spurs attached to his boots. As soon as the king permitted, Ederyn returned to the Castle of Content to woo the lily maiden.

After he returned to Camelot with his bride, he created a family crest to symbolize his many years of faithfulness. He emblazoned on his shield and helmet the symbol of his destiny: A crest with a heart and a hand that grasped a spear and the words, "Be faithful or die!"

THE ENCHANTED NECKLACE

Once upon a time, there lived an old woman, or *babushka*, named Svetlana. She lived in the woods near a great, turreted castle in the Ural Mountains and had been a beauty in her day. Years before, she had been married but a week when her husband was sent off to war under the forces of the Tsar, never to return. Left to her own resources, Svetlana found a small thatched cottage about a mile from the castle and searched about for a way to make a living. She learned how to spin fibers from the blue-flowered flax plant into linen cloth and so earned enough to live on. One day, as she gathered flowers in the woods, she came upon a baby girl abandoned beneath a tree. Having no children, Svetlana took the infant home, named her Olga, and raised her as her own.

Every morning, Olga performed errands for the old woman: carrying water from the spring, gathering wild berries from the bushes and spreading the linen cloth on the grass to bleach. She had a good and grateful heart and the old woman heartily hoped she could find a good man and settle into more prosperous surroundings than what Svetlana had been able to give her. They lived a simple life, the two of them, but Svetlana feared for her young charge if someday the babushka's tired heart gave out.

One day, Olga had gone down to the spring to search for watercress when the prince of the castle rode by on his dashing black horse. A snow-white plume was stuck in his royal blue hat. Being in the last stage of a long journey back home, Prince Pavel was thirsty and tired and desiring a drink. Seeing there was no cup or dipper with which to drink, Olga held her hands under the cold stream coming out of the earth and gathered a handful of water. Standing up, she offered him the sparkling water from her hands, doing so in such a graceful manner that the prince was charmed by her humility and modesty and eagerly drank from her uplifted hands. He asked her name and where she lived, thanked her, then rode away.

The next day, a palace courier in red and gold silk stopped at the door of the cottage with an invitation to the castle for Olga. A series of seven balls were to be given there on seven nights and Olga's presence was requested at each one. The old flax-spinner beamed at the sight of the invitation and promised the courier Olga would attend.

"But why," Olga cried out after he had ridden away, "did you promise him I'd be there when you know full well I only have one dress and that of brown linen, which is at best a beggar's clothing? Better that I stay here than be ashamed in front of all those guests."

"Don't worry, my child," Svetlana replied. "You shall have the finest of ball gowns. I have worked for years for this day to arrive, for I love you as though you were my own daughter."

Leaving Olga, the old woman went into an inner room and pricked herself with the sharp point of the spindle atop her spinning wheel until a large drop of blood fell into her trembling hand. She blew on it and the drop shrank into a tiny round ball like a seed, which she strung on a thread along with 76 other beads. For years she had been saving her life's blood for such an occasion and now she had reached 77, the number of perfection.

A week later, it was the night of the first ball and Olga had already combed her long, golden hair and intertwined it with snow-white water lilies. To her astonishment, the old woman brought to her not a marvelous ball gown but a string of dark red beads, which she clasped around Olga's throat. Olga could not help weeping in disappointment.

"Obey me and all shall be well," the old woman promised. "When you reach the gates of the castle, clasp one bead in your fingers and say:

"For love's sweet sake, in my hour of need,
"Blossom and clothe me, little seed."

"And then you shall be clothed in the most beautiful of gowns. You have been a good daughter to me and this is how I reward you. But memorize those words, for only to the words "for love's sweet sake," will the necklace produce its treasures. If you forget, you will only be left with your brown linen dress."

So Olga ran through the moonlit night through the forest until she reached the castle gate. She paused and, grasping one of the beads, repeated the charm:

> *"For love's sweet sake, in my hour of need,*
> *"Blossom and clothe me, little seed."*

Immediately the bead burst with a red, smoky puff, a faint perfume surrounded her and Olga found her brown linen dress transformed into a filmy pink gown that looked so delicate, it could have been a cloud. The white lilies in her hair had become pink roses. She entered through the gate and followed the crowds to the ballroom, causing the prince to sit up on his throne in amazement when he saw her. That entire night, Pavel had eyes only for her for, "Surely," he told all the others, "some rose from heaven drifted down here tonight."

The next night, Olga appeared at the castle gate in her brown linen dress and once again clasping a bead in her fingers, said:

> *"For love's sweet sake, in my hour of need,*
> *"Blossom and clothe me, little seed."*

The seed vanished in a red 'pouf' and this time, Olga was clothed in pale daffodil yellow, her hair covered with tiny diamonds. All who saw her likened her to the legendary golden firebird that lives in the frozen steppes and forests of the Russian north. That night, the prince complimented her so highly and paid her so much attention that she became proud and wished she could forget the humble cottage in which she had grown up. The next day, when she was back to wearing her linen dress, she complained at her lot in life and resented having to pick fruit, gather wood and carry water. Finally, she sat down by the spring and moped, refusing to spread the linen on the grass to bleach.

The old flax-spinner's fingers trembled as she spun that day, for she could see the change in her adopted daughter's face and guessed at Olga's discontentment at having to do the tasks of a servant after having had two glorious nights at the castle. She had given of her heart's blood to buy happiness for the girl and knew that one brief moment of pride could mean the loss of everything for Olga. Had she, the old woman wondered, sacrificed her precious blood in vain?

Olga returned to the castle that night, but a full day of complaining had caused her to forget the verse. Nevertheless, she grasped the necklace. "Clothe me at once!" she commanded. "Make me lovelier than any woman has ever been so that I may finally win the prince's heart and become a bride in his castle. Then I shall no more have to bother with spinning and weaving."

But the moon went behind a cloud and a the wind began to moan around the turrets. The black night hawks in the forest flapped their wings as a warning and black bats began to hover about her head.

"Obey me at once!" she cried angrily, stamping her foot and jerking at the necklace. The string broke and the beads went rolling in all directions and were lost, all but one, which she clasped in her hand. Then Olga fell to the ground and wept in her plain brown linen dress in the darkness. As her sobbing died down, she thought she heard the night wind: "Hush!" it seemed to say. "A heart can never come to harm if lips but speak the old woman's charm."

The night wind sounded so much like the voice of her beloved babushka that Olga looked about, half expecting to see the old woman standing there. Instead she saw the thatched cottage and then the old woman's bent back, patiently spinning flax at her spinning wheel so she and the girl might have food. All the years in which the good Svetlana had toiled her her seemed to march before Olga and reproach her with a list of a thousand kind things the woman had done. "How could you forget, Olga?" they seemed to say. "Her good deeds were done for love's sweet sake and that alone."

Then Olga realized how proud she had become and she began crying again. Strangely enough, her tears seemed to make her eyesight better, as if only now she could see that no power of her own could have produced such lovely dresses; that only someone else's love and sacrifice had made them hers. Suddenly she remembered the charm and, holding onto her one last bead, she repeated it, this time humbly:

> *"For love's sweet sake, in my hour of need,*
> *"Blossom and deck me, little seed."*

The words had no sooner come out of her lips than the moon came out from behind the clouds, the fragrance of lilies was around her and she found herself dressed in a fair white dress, covered with lace. A veil, decked with pearls, cascaded down from her blond hair. She appeared at the castle door looking so dazzling that the prince knelt before her, kissed her hand and proclaimed her his bride in front of all the guests. He summoned the bishop who led the crowd to the church on castle grounds. There, the flax-spinner's daughter became Princess Olga, the wife of Prince Pavel.

The celebrations lasted throughout the rest of the seven days and in the merriment, Princess Olga once again forgot the motherly old woman; how kind she had been and how lonely she now was with no one to help her. But the beads that had rolled away into the darkness buried themselves in the earth and sprang up by the castle gate. They appeared as strange red flowers, for on every stem hung a row of little bleeding hearts.

Seeing them from her window, Princess Olga went down to investigate what sort of flower they were. "What are you?" she asked them, for in all her wanderings about the forest, she had never encountered these.

"We bloom for love's sweet sake," they told her. "We have sprung from the old flax-spinner's gift, the necklace that you in your impatience broke and scattered. From her heart's blood she gave this to you and her heart still bleeds to think you have now forgotten her."

Then they told the princess of all the old woman's 77 sacrifices, how each time she had experienced pain as she had given blood. Princess Olga was overcome with remorse at how once again, she had forgotten such a great kindness. Summoning her husband, she showed him the flowers, then took him to the thatched cottage where they found the old flax-spinner and brought her to the castle to live the rest of her life in comfort.

But the flowers we call bleeding hearts remain to this day, blooming where discerning eyes may see them, reminding us how often we find our happiness because other people's hearts that bleed for love's sweet sake.

THE JESTER'S SWORD

He was born in March, the month the ancient Romans attributed to Mars, the red planet of war. His people were proud Scots, scattered about the chilly highlands of their country, gathering often to display their proud tartans and engage in their war games or defending their territory against the English and whoever else would threaten them. When his mother the queen first saw how her squalling son had come out of the womb with a full head of red curls, she gave him a name not as a chieftan but as red star: Aldebaran, in the constellation of Taurus, the bull. Because he was born in Mars' month, he was given a special ring, a signet ring with a bloodstone in it, a token that unfailing courage would be the jewel that symbolized his soul.

He had six brothers, and all of them were as strong and fit as he and each one, it was said, was capable of mighty, valiant deeds. All were surpassingly good at the yearly contests of saber tossing, putting the stone, tossing the sheaf and throwing the hammer that enlivened their lives. Yet, of Aldebaran, whose birth was marked by the auspicious appearance of a comet that lit up the late winter skies, it was foretold that his would be the greatest destiny of any of them. From the time he was an infant, it was known that the Sword of Conquest should belong to him. This sword had passed down through the ages from father to son down a line of kings. It was not always given to the oldest one, as was the throne, but to the one toward whom all the celestial signs pointed as being worthiest of it.

Thus the sword was destined for Aldebaran from the time he lay in his wooden cradle and so it became his greatest teacher. His old nurse encouraged him with such tales of it that even as he played and frolicked, the thought of such a noble heritage moved him to dare greater risks

41

than his friends even thought of doing. He knelt many nights by his window, gazing at the reddish star after which he was named, as it wheeled overhead him in the azure heavens. In his heart he whispered the words that the eldest of the clan—a man with the gift of prophecy—had said at his baptism: "As Aldebaran the star shines in the heavens, so Aldebaran the man shall shine among his fellows."

Day after day, his ambition to excel among his brothers grew within him until it was as much a part of his every thought as the strong heart beating in his breast. Only to one person did he express such hopes and her name was Vesta, his childhood playmate. Born several weeks before him, on Feb. 29, a leap year day that occurs only once every four years, she too was an unusual child since her birth. As they held the newborn infant, her startled parents noticed that the child's hair was almost white. Each year, as she grew, it turned silver, as if to portray great wisdom beyond the normal scope of her age.

When Aldebaran confided to her the words of the prophecy spoken over him, she repeated a similiar foretelling of her own destiny: "As Vesta the star keeps watch in the heavens above the dwellings of mortals, so Vesta the maiden shall keep eternal vigil beside he who is the bravest of all men." When Aldebaran heard that, he swore by his bloodstone ring that when he was old enough to wield his sword, he would show the world an unsurpassed courage. And Vesta smiled, promising to keep vigil by one fire only, the fire she had kindled in his heart.

One by one, his six older brothers grew up and went out into the world to seek their fortunes while Aldebaran gazed restlessly after them, like a restless stallion kept penned up in a stall. It was time, he thought, to prove his bravery and keep his vow to be the most courageous of all men. Only in that way, he thought, could Vesta's and his destinies be linked together.

Finally the day came for his father to present him with the Sword of Conquest. The king had bypassed his other sons to award the awesome gift to his youngest child, for he, like his entire court, saw the greatness inherent in the lad. One day, during the annual gathering of the clans, Aldebaran was summoned to stand before the castle gates. Bagpipes blared and a long line of nobles filed through, followed by his father walking to the sound of cheers and the ringing of bells. Surrounding him were his strongest fighting men in their ceremonial tartans. As he saw the dignified sovereign, Aldebaran knelt to receive his blessing. A ray of morning light suddenly shown on the king, who laid his hands on his son's bowed head and said with great insight:

"A king's son you are and always will be,
"As you take up the sword and your enemies flee.
"You'll fulfill your destiny when you take part
"In defeating the enemy that threatens your heart."

It was a mysterious word and the king did not explain it. Instead, he handed Aldebaran the Sword of Conquest as the crowd roared.

"I swear," Aldebaran said, when the cheering had died down, "that until I make a braver conquest than has ever been made before, I shall not return home. By the bloodstone on my finger I promise this!"

The crowd whispered and wondered at what great deed he might perform. Maybe, some said, he would be the one to entrap the Loch Ness monster, that mysterious half-dragon, half-fish that prowled the depths of the country's deepest lake. The king knew that his son would keep his promise beyond what anyone else expected of him, for weren't the stars his witness and example? So Aldebaran mounted his black horse and rode off, gazing back only once to see Vesta sorrowfully standing at her window, waving farewell. His heart was struck for unless he kept his oath, he would never see her again.

It seemed at first that Aldebaran would make good with his promise within a year, as he defeated every monster and enemy brought to his attention and his name was sung by every troubadour in the British Isles. Wherever he went, to Ireland or France or even far-off Spain, he was known and spoken of at every court. Tales of his bravery regularly made their way back to his father's court, as Aldebaran was unbeatable by every foe. No weakness, no sickness could happen to him; defeat was unknown to him as he wrestled against tyrants, giants, dragons and other monsters. His Sword of Conquest was frequently used to win his victories and he began wondering if there were not some greater enemy he could vanquish. He began to picture his homecoming and Vesta dressed in bridal finery, the city paving his triumphant entrance with rose petals. Never did he think it would happen otherwise, for hadn't the prophet foretold that his success would rival the stars?

One night, after a day of wandering through the purple heather moors, he took shelter during a storm underneath a rock in a mountain pass, wrapping his cape about him as he lay down to sleep. Perhaps tomorrow he would find a great monster to slay, he thought, and after that long and glorious battle, he would start wending his way home again. But in the darkest watches of the night, fierce winds swept down the mountainside with great fury, uprooting centuries-old trees and sweeping great rocks into an avalanche. Aldebaran lay in its path as the earth bore down on him and swept him up, pinning him beneath a large fallen tree. He lay there until the next morning, as if dead, until two passing goatherders found him, hoisted him on their backs and with great pity bore him to their *shieling* hut nearby, used for summer grazing.

He was wracked with a fever and in great pain for weeks, but when at last he crawled out of the hut into the sunshine, he found he had become a mishapen creature, maimed and marred with a twisted back, a face contorted into a grimace and a foot that dragged. His sword arm hung nerveless by his side. Never again would it draw the Sword of Conquest. He lacked even the strength to draw it from its bejeweled scabbard.

Making his way to a pond in a nearby glen, he bent over and gazed at his reflection in horror, as it seemed as if some hideous nightmare had taken hold of him. "This is not I," he thought and then as the truth began to pierce his soul and the specter of a wasted life lay before him, he still denied it: "This is not I!" he groaned. He said it again and again, as if by saying the words he could work a miracle and be restored to his former self. Finally, an understanding of his true predicament swept over him like a flood and he threw himself on the ground, praying to die. But death chose not to come, waiting for him to rise and grapple with this last and greatest foe, this greatest enemy of his heart. Only in conquering this could the possibility of cowardice be wiped from his soul.

This was Aldebaran's terrible choice. At first he could not endure the thought of his now useless life and, like a broken-winged, drooping eagle, he lurked inside the *shieling* hut, weeping and cursing the remaining strength within him that kept him alive. To fall asleep with the world at his feet, then to wake up empty-handed in this living nightmare was agony. His once invincible arms now lacked strength; his fate, once set among the stars, doomed him to creep about the earth like a poor, crushed worm. Now, he was the target for everyone's pity, whereas before he was the focus of everyone's admiration.

He thought of Vesta most of all, for the stroke that robbed him of his strength and handsome looks had surely robbed him of her as well. It had been said that she shall "keep eternal vigil beside he is who is bravest of all men" and he had not risen above the level of his ancestors' bravery, only up to it. Now, weak as he was, it would be impossible to show the world a greater courage. Even if she would get word of his condition and come to him out of pity to share his ruined life, he could not accept it. His pride would not allow even a sign of pity from her in whose sight he only wanted to be strong. This was a pain greater than any that wracked his tortured arms and legs. As though he was casting heaven far from him, he drew his tattered cape close about him, hiding his disfigurement as best as he might and prayed that Vesta might never see him like this.

As the days wore on, he realized he was imposing on the goatsherders' hospitality for food was scarce and they were sharing what they had with him. One evening he bade them thanks and farewell, walking down the mountainside to the village, hoping under the cover of dusk he could find a chance to earn a little money. As he neared the little town where the sound of the bells on the sheep coming home and the lighted candles in each window brought memories of a time when all ears and eyes would have been on his glorious entrance, he sank into despair. Once upon a time, every window in this hamlet would have blazed for him. Every door would have been flung open wide to welcome Aldebaran, the royal Scottish prince, bearer of the Sword of Conquest. And now he was a crippled excuse of a man, whose twisted features were enough to set the dogs at his heels.

"In all the world," he said to himself, "there breathes no other man who has suffered such a cruel fate! Emptied of hope and robbed of everything I love, my very body has become a dungeon. Why should I struggle any longer? What keeps me from lying here and starving? At least death would deliver me from this indignity."

As he mused, he heard footsteps coming his way and a hearty male voice belting out a song. Before he could duck into the bushes, a head bearing a jaunty multi-colored striped cap appeared above the underbrush. It was the village jester, skipping along the path as if he had not a care in the world. Suddenly he saw Aldebaran and jerked to a stop. He leaned closer and quickly made the sign of the cross as though to protect himself. Aldebaran shrank back. He must look worse than he had thought.

But within that jester's outfit was a wise, sympathetic man whose motto, written across his heart was: "To ease the burden of the world." Somehow he had managed to persuade everyone he met that their problems were truly light and of how fortunate they truly were. So he stood and gazed upon the cowering Aldebaran, who hid his face in the crook of his arms, refusing to even look up.

"What ails you, brother?" the jester asked, seating himself on the grass. Although Aldebaran had resolved not to repeat his tale, the unexpected, saintly sympathy of the jester won him over. The jester did not add to Aldebaran's sorrows by showing him pity or loading blame upon him. Instead, he talked in the most playful of tones, as if Aldebaran's sorrows were but the most passing of woes and would soon vanish. Finally, when he had heard Aldebaran's tale, he began to laugh.

"Although I'm supposed to be the fool and you the wise man, I think it's the other way around," he said. "Gadzooks! Look at you, man! Here you go traveling about the world, eager to find a chance to show unequalled courage and when at last the dear Lord shoves it under your very nose, you turn away! Get up! Know this: It takes a thousand times more courage to sheathe the sword when one is all on fire for action than to go forth against the greatest foe. Here is your chance to show the world the most noble and kingly spirit it has ever seen.

"For it is easy to rejoice and love life when you are healthy and have everything you want," he said. "It is so much harder to struggle daily with hurts that prick you to the quick and to do without the blessings everyone else takes for granted. This sheathed sword at your side will stab you hourly with memories of what you once were and with far deeper thrusts than any enemy could give you. But you must counter that with hope of the noble man you will become. It is a fight until death. Are you brave enough to take this gauntlet that Despair flings at your feet and wage this warfare until heaven calls you home to your reward?"

Aldebaran gazed at his twisted arms, then caught sight of the bloodstone ring that remained upon his gnarled hand and hope leapt up in his kingly soul.

"I'll keep my oath," he said, struggling to his feet and laying his hand on the jeweled hilt by his side. "By this sheathed sword, since the blade is denied me, I will shine among my fellow man as was prophesied about me." Suddenly, all things seemed possible. The jester had given him the gift of hope. Limping behind his new friend, he followed the jester to his thatched roof home, where a great fire blazed on the fireplace and the jester brought him a warm drink, loaves of wheat bread and meat roasting on the spit. They sat and talked for awhile and then the jester leaned forward and took a closer look at his guest.

"The wind that blew you from your course may send me on my way rejoicing," he said. "For many years I've long wished to leave this cold country and journey to the south, where my cousins live. But there was never anyone to replace me. Whenever I have mentioned leaving, the townspeople here have refused to let me go. It's as bad, they say, as if the priest left, with no one to shepherd his flock. Well, this whole town is my flock. `Who will help relieve our sadness?' they ask me. `Who will cheer us up?' `Who will help us bear our troubles by making us forget them?' 'You cannot leave us, Mr. Jester, until some other merry soul comes along who reminds us to dance and sing when we are sad.' And now, you are here."

"Oh, to be sure," Aldebaran replied sarcastically, "as if I have every reason to be merry at this time in my life."

"Well," his host admitted, "you're not there yet but at least you could act the part. You could at least put on my jester's garb and learn the jokes by which I help these poor people laugh. You won't be the first person who's hid an aching heart behind a smile. Here, take this pipe! The tune you play may not bring you pleasure but if it makes people want to dance and sing, it is enough. Besides, it is an honest and honorable way to earn your daily bread. Have you a better idea of how to do so?

Aldebaran hid his face in his hands and groaned. "Not at all," he said. "There is no other way out, yet I cannot stand the thought of myself, a king's son, descending to such a low estate. How can I put on the jester's cap and bells?"

"Because you are a king's son," the Jester explained. "That, more than any other, is reason why you should play more royally than other men."

Aldebaran sat wrapped in thought for a long time. He remembered his father's words when he gave him the Sword of Conquest; something about fighting against the enemy that threatened his heart. And now the beast of depression and melancholy sat at his door. "Well," he finally said, "I guess a 100 hundred years from now, my troubles will seem quite little and people will judge me for how I reacted to them. Good friend, I accept your offer with gratitude."

The next morning, the two set off into the marketplace. Aldebaran hid behind a painted mask and showed a brave front to the crowd. No one guessed at the misery within him nor of the mental effort it took to imitate the Jester and play the fool before the crowds. He hated doing it, yet being raised in the royal court had given him discernment and he was quick to perceive peoples' thoughts. To the humble peasants who gathered around him, his perceptive words seemed like magic to them. And his pipe seemed like heaven itself; the music a memory of high, kingly deeds and the unfurling of banners and the calling forth of destinies. Just hearing the notes made everyone stand straighter and prouder. The Jester was quite pleased, for his pupil had surpassed his teacher on the first day of his training. He was already counting the days until he could travel south when the two returned to the thatched cottage and Aldebaran tore off his mask and threw himself on the ground.

"I cannot endure this!" he cried out. "All day long I've not been able to forget what I have lost and it's been sheer agony being the target of peoples' pointing fingers and their laughter. When I saw two young lovers chasing each other down the lane, I nearly went mad. How can I endure such sights day after day when my arms will remain empty? How can I listen to children play when I shall never know a son's caress? My dear rescuer, this was a sad choice."

The Jester gazed on Aldebaran's drawn, white face and said nothing, but kindled a fire and fixed two steaming bowls of soup.

"At any rate," he responded, "you've kept your promise for one full day. Even though your walk through the village has cost you dearly, you've held despair away from you for a full day. Why, it was the bravest thing you've ever done. If you could last through today, why not tomorrow? We are called to endure only one hour at a time. By the bloodstone that's your birthright, promise me you'll keep your promise one more day."

Aldebaran assented and slowly one day followed another until two weeks has passed by. Because he did not complain, the Jester once again thought of traveling to see his cousins and supposed Aldebaran's struggle had grown easier.

"Don't leave me yet," said Aldebaran, guessing his thoughts. "You are my only crutch and it is your cheerful presence that gives me the courage to live another day."

"Yet, you will show greater courage when you can face your fate alone," the Jester said. "Here, take this string that I have used for fishing. Create with it a memory string of beads that symbolize good deeds and thanks to God for the blessings you do have. Despair cannot be defeated until you teach yourself to feel the gladness that you only pretend to have now. Counting your blessings will help you forget your losses."

The next day, Aldebaran took his string with him as he went for a walk early that morning. As he gave thanks to God for the sun, the birds and the green grass, he slipped three beads on his string.

"I should be glad for bread, for fresh water and the power to smell the budding purple lilacs by the door and for friendly villagers," he said to himself. By the time he came home that night, a long string of beads was on the string. As last he's found the cure, the Jester thought, before Aldebaran flung the beads from him and covered his face with his hands.

"This will drive me mad!" he cried. "How can I string beads that only remind me of all that I have lost? May heaven forgive me but the truth is: I am not glad. This is all just a mockery."

By then, the Jester had run out of ideas on how to console his crippled friend. The two men sat in silence until they heard a knock at the door. The visitor was an old Franciscan friar begging for money for the poor and the Jester let him in. He invited the friar to stay for dinner, as their meal was almost ready. The friar, who was hungry as well, pulled up a chair to the table and devoured the fish and soup they had on hand, all the time cheerfully talking about his life. Aldebaran gazed at him, amazed.

"Surely your life is hard, good friar," he finally said, looking curiously into the man's wrinkled face. "Every day you humble yourself to beg from door to door, giving up what you wish so that the poor may be fed but still, you seem so joyful. What is your secret and how have you found true happiness?"

"By never searching for it," the friar answered. "I learned that lesson from the stars. Many years ago I lived in a monastery where I was restless and unhappy with my family's choice to put me there while I was yet a boy, with never the chance to choose a wife like other men have had. One night the abbot took me outside underneath the stars. He pointed to the glittering heavens and told me that God had appointed a duty for me. If I stepped aside from the path He had chosen for me, it would alter the order of God's universe as if a star had dropped from its place.

"'You do not shine with your own light,' he told me, `but neither do the planets contain light. They all shine with the reflected glory of the sun. And so will you, staying faithful to your orbit, reflect the light of heaven upon this world's unhappy ways.'

"Since then, I never felt the need to seek my own happiness," the friar continued, "for bringing happiness to others keeps my heart light. And so I pass on this lesson, my good host. Remember, people need laughter sometimes more than food and even if you have none of your own to give, go gather it from door to door as I gather food, carrying what you find to those who need it."

Long after the friar had departed, Aldebaran sat and thought. Then crossing over to a tiny window, he gazed up at the stars and mulled over the prophecy.

"As Aldebaran the star shines in the heavens," he said to himself, "so Aldebaran the man will shine among his fellows. This is my destiny: to reflect the light and beauty of God to all who need it."

From that day on, the Jester noticed a change in his guest, for Aldebaran no longer avoided the happy scenes about the village. Instead, he sought them out, knowing that if he would shed joy on others, he must first go to where he could find some. Even though the thought of giving up Vesta drove him to tears, he sheathed his dreams of her in his mind just as he had sheathed his legendary sword. Once a little child came crying toward him in the marketplace, crying because his toy was broken. Beforehand, Aldebaran would have turned away, reminded of how he was being denied the joy of fatherhood. But now he stooped gently to wipe the boy's tears away. When he had fixed the toy and given it to the child, he was rewarded with a wet kiss. Aldebaran's heart was so warmed that when, a few minutes later, he met a man who had lost all his possessions, he did not respond bitterly as he once would have done. Instead, he spoke of the treasures life still held for this man so that within the hour, the man was comforted. The man's grateful smile was like a sudden revelation to Aldebaran. Indeed, he thought, he did have such power as only belongs to the stars. For despite the lack of joy in his own life, he could reflect God's joy and bring hope and cheer to others.

Months, then years passed and when the Jester had finally left to go south, no one missed him because Aldebaran so deftly filled his place. The townspeople eventually forgot there had been another Jester and Aldebaran began to feel the gladness that he had only pretended to have before. For wherever he went, he brought hope with him and a sense of heaven's presence and willingness to help.

Finally, 20 years had passed since that awful storm and Aldebaran's maimed body gave out at last. Just before he died, he confided to the priest his true identity and so it was with great sorrow the villagers formed a procession to return Aldebaran to his father's castle several weeks' journey away. They found the Sword of Conquest hidden underneath his cloak where it had stayed still all these years and they marveled that he had carried such a treasure, yet had told no one of it. His father had long given up his son for dead and great had been the mourning at the castle; yet one spring day a herald arrived at the palace to say a great procession was on the way.

"What noble man is dead that the people do him such honor?" the old king asked.

"It's but our Jester who they say was your youngest son," the herald replied. "He was a poor, maimed creature on the outside but he bore his misfortune with such grace that it seemed like a kingly spirit lived among us. Now we have learned he was a prince and the earth is poorer after his passing."

When the funeral procession finally arrived at the castle gate, the king and his six sons came to meet it. Aldebaran's story was written all over his face; how through great suffering he had kept his promise. His jester's cap and costume seemed more majestic, more regal than the richest crown. The sheathed sword told of years of inward struggle more precious than the blood of many dragons and on his face there was a peace that came from having triumphed.

The king stayed long by his son's side, not speaking.

"Bring royal purple for the casket," he finally said, "and leave the Sword of Conquest on him. No other hands will be found more worthy to claim it, for he has conquered despair, the greatest foe this world contains."

They placed his body on a royal bier in the cathedral, surrounded by tall white candles, where all the people could come and see where nobility lay. Late that night, a woman approached the bier, dressed in a bridal veil and wedding gown. It was Vesta, her silver hair done up like a queen, who had kept herself all these years for her groom. She knelt beside him, her face filled with starry light, the two children named after the stars finally being one. All who watched her drew back in awe at the sight as a soft radiance filled the nave.

"It's as the prophet foretold," they whispered. "Her soul has entered on its deathless vigil for he was the bravest man this earth has ever known."

PRINCESS WINSOME AND

THE JADE DRAGON

Many dynasties ago in China, a prince and a princess lived in a beautiful ivory palace on the Yellow Sea. Princess Winsome, who had just turned seventeen, had a face like the moon. Her younger brother, Prince Wisdom, had a face like the sun, and together they were as happy as could be. Their lives included many delights, not the least of which was gazing at the sea from the palace's exquisite teak balconies. Every evening, as they strolled on those balconies to gaze at the bamboo gardens below or at the moon above, the servants would light elegant paper lanterns, one by one, until the palace was ablaze.

Lantern festivals were held on every full moon, and on those nights, the children could stay up late and walk about with their own lanterns. Or they could play with the many royal peacocks who strutted about the palace grounds, preening their feathers and showing off their finery. And every New Year, the Emperor would order the grandest fireworks to be set off. People would journey for days just to see the lovely explosions against the dark skies above the palace.

The princess knew that soon her father, the Emperor, would be scouring the kingdom for a suitable husband for her, and then she must leave her lovely seaside palace. But for now, she thought not of it. Instead, she learned how to play the zither, use the abacus, and cultivate silkworms. From these she spun fine silk, which she then dyed in rich colors and wove into complex fabrics. Her brother was far less industrious, preferring to chase the peacocks about the gardens, sip ginseng tea with his friends, and occasionally dip a brush in ink to trace out elaborate Chinese characters. He loved parties, especially if they were for him.

Everything changed one cool spring day, as the plum tree blossoms were just appearing on the branches of a thousand plum trees that surrounded the palace. It was close to the Birthday of a Hundred Flowers, a spring festival celebrated by everyone in that seaside kingdom. But that day, the Empress noticed something strange in her morning tea. In her tea leaves the pattern of a dragon appeared, a threatening green monster that glowered at her, then disappeared. Some instinct told her that danger was imminent, and she rushed out to the balcony to check the grounds for signs of her children.

Prince Wisdom was playing on the nearby beach, collecting conch shells and playing with turtles. Yet a long distance off was a dot that blotted the morning sky. *Could it be a bird?* the Empress wondered. The creature flew nearer. The Empress stood transfixed, for this was not a bird but a flying dragon, and a green one at that. Her morning tea had turned into a living nightmare. She cried out. Hearing her scream, Princess Winsome rushed out to the balcony where she, too, saw the approaching menace. The girl flew down the steps to the grass and ran toward the beach to warn her unsuspecting brother.

But the dragon was flying very quickly, and in less than a minute was circling over the two children. By this time, the Emperor and his guards had come out to the balcony, just in time to see the jade-colored monster swoop down toward the beach. With one claw he scooped up the prince, and with the other, clasped the princess to his scaly chest. The guards dared not fire arrows at the monster for fear that the children would be harmed. Clutching his screaming prey, the jade dragon lifted slowly into the sky, breathed a trail of fire toward the horrified onlookers on the balcony, then headed southwest, toward the mountains.

The dragon and the children flew and flew toward the roof of the world, where the snow-covered peaks seemed to cover the sky, and where cold winds buffeted the dreary lands still encased in winter. Nestled in that place was a beautiful valley, where bright tropical flowers bloomed, and palm trees waved gently in a warm breeze. Here lived the Tiger Lady, who loved to bring down ruin on whomever she could. It was she who had sent her pet dragon out to bring back those who would soon become her servants.

The dragon approached the valley and landed just outside the orchard, leaving both the prince and princess crumpled in the grass.

"Hail, Queen of all Tigers," the dragon said. Secretly he detested this woman, but he was too afraid to do anything but pay her the most fawning compliments.

She turned and gazed at the captured children.

"The royal son and daughter!" she exulted. "Had you not returned with such choice victims, I might have ended your life."

"You told me to head for the palace," the jade creature said. "Seeing it reminded me of my fair home, where I lived before I was brought here."

"Forget those days," the Tiger Lady snapped. "You've chosen children with powerful friends. It will be a while before they find us here, but they will come. When they do, we'll make sure the children are so changed that they will never be recognized and never return to the palace."

The princess called out, "I warn you, old woman, that if you harm us in any way, our father the Emperor will repay you!"

But the Tiger Lady dragged them away to a tall stone tower in the midst of a vast orchard. The tower had a winding stair and a tiny room at the top with one small window. Into this room she thrust them and shut the door behind them with a clang. She then pulled out a long key and locked the door.

Then the Tiger Lady filled a cup with a clear red liquid, which she handed to the dragon. There seemed to be some holy protection about the princess, she said, but the prince was younger and more vulnerable. When the prince and princess were asleep, he must pour this drop by drop on the prince's tongue. Because the prince was royalty, he could not be turned into just any beast, but instead he would become a noble one: a chow chow, a lion-like dog entrusted with guarding Chinese nobility. Then she added a warning:

> To keep the prince within my grasp,
> Make sure he does not get free.
> For if he eats seven silver plums
> From any one plum tree,
> He shall become a prince again
> And destroy our villainy

Meanwhile, many miles away, the Emperor and Empress wept as they explained the awful news of the kidnapping to the Lady Qing, the children's only aunt, and sister to the Empress. She was also godmother to Princess Winsome. As a child, Lady Qing and her brother had also been kidnapped. Her brother, Lord Jade, had disappeared and was never seen again. But she was rescued by fairies, who promised their help the rest of her life as long as she dedicated her life to doing good. The Lady Qing agreed to this arrangement and in return received a special gift of wisdom and knowledge of things unseen. Perhaps it was the glint of her ice blue eyes that gave away her deep wisdom, or perhaps it was her delicate hands that held a pale pink fan in front of her.

"Do you know," she asked the worried couple, "what the Tiger Lady has already done to your son?" They shook their heads. She smiled.

"Your children are in a room in a high tower," the exquisite woman said, "far to the south of you. Your daughter is lying next to a large, furry dog, which I believe was your son a few moments ago. He has been changed by that wicked old woman."

"No!" the couple said.

"Your son has not become just any dog, but part of a noble breed— the blue-tongued chow chow, who in ages past has always guarded the imperial family."

"What shall we do?" the parents asked.

"You can't help them," Lady Qing said. "Your daughter, though, has the means to work out her rescue if she is obedient and diligent. I shall visit her right away. I shall go to the tower under the cover of night carrying raw silk and a spinning wheel for the princess. Meanwhile, you must seek a champion to rescue them both. Take heart, for remember:

She'll sing and spin her golden thread
In the moon's bright ray,
The spinning wheel your grief shall heal,
For love will find a way.

Off she went, with a burst of red stars, as the parents shook their heads, wondering what she meant.

"I will send messengers throughout my domain," the Emperor said, "proclaiming that any warrior who rescues my children shall marry my daughter." As they sat down to dinner, the Emperor was already composing his decree.

Soon after their meal, one of their servants came up to say a man awaited them in the hall and would like to speak to them. The man was summoned.

He was dressed as a warrior, in a bright-colored tunic and trousers with a short sword by his side. Beside him was a round shield. He told them he was Lord Xing, from China's far western steppes.

"It is a pleasure," said the Emperor, "to have friends come from afar."

The warrior bowed. "A man full of faith is respected wherever he goes," he said. "Lady Qing has already told me of your situation."

"You know of my sister?" the Empress asked.

"Those who follow the Heavenly Emperor always know each other," the man replied, "even when separated by time and space. To find your children will be an easy matter," he added, "but to win the heart of your daughter may be far more difficult."

"How so?" the father asked.

"She is known far and wide for her good heart," the warrior said, "and for her lovely silks. They say of her:

> *This we learned from the shadow of a tree*
> *That sways to and fro on the wall—*
> *That where the princess may never be,*
> *Her influence does fall.*
> *Someday her shadow shall unbind*
> *The cruelest imprisonment of them all.*

"Amazing!" said the Empress. "Can it be that such a prophecy is spoken of our own daughter?"

"I always knew she was special," the Emperor said. "Tell us, Lord Xing, can you bring them back?"

"The Lady Qing has already told me where they are," the warrior replied. "Before this moon is full, I'll return victorious from this quest. Yet first I must find a flute made of pearl hidden near the Great Wall. It will summon hundreds of powerful fairy folk who will aid me in this mission. Love will find a way, and with your blessing, I am off."

"May you succeed," the Emperor cried, waving farewell. "Remember that inside his heart, the warrior keeps to the ways of peace. Outside his heart, he keeps his weapons ready for use."

They watched him ride away as the sun set and up rose the moon. Meanwhile, that same golden, glistening orb that lit their night sky sent its beams down many miles away on a mournful princess. Her eyes were red from crying, and her arms were wrapped about a large dog built like a small lion. Beside the two was a bowl of cold rice left there by the dragon.

"Why," she asked, "are you in such a shape? Don't turn those sad eyes on me. I see no escape from this evil woman's power in the long hours we've been gone. Why, our parents must think we're dead! They weep this very hour. What a cruel fate! What's that noise I hear? Oh, Wisdom, if you could only speak! For outside the door, I hear someone coming."

The door opened and there stood the Lady Qing, glowing with an inner light. In her arms were piles of silk, ready to be spun into thread, and behind her, a spinning wheel.

"Dry your teary eyes and get to work," she said. "The only way you'll escape this awful place is through the work of your own hands. Don't waste your time in sorrows. Spin and sing instead. For the way out of your prison lies in this golden thread."

"How so?" the princess asked.

"See this spinning wheel?" replied Lady Qing. "Now, use it! Forget your problems of the past and keep this wheel spinning well and fast."

"How did you get in here?" asked the princess.

"There are heavenly powers you know nothing of," the godmother said. "Someday I'll tell you. But for now, don't delay in obeying me. For by the time the next full moon rises, the Tiger Lady will try to kill you. This thread is your hope of rescue."

"How is that?" the princess asked. "How can a golden thread release me from this tower?"

"I cannot tell you that," Lady Qing replied. "You must trust that I know what is best. But I will tell you that your rescuer even now searches for a flute of pearl to summon the fairies to set you free. Messengers shall tell you more. Now, why have you not kept up your strength by eating the rice provided you?"

"I am used to eating my rice with fish and peanuts," the princess said. "This is plain and dry."

"There are no fish in these parts," her godmother said, "and you will not be treated like royalty here. She who is impatient over trifles will make mistakes in major enterprises. Take what you are given and never forgo an opportunity to learn virtue." She disappeared in a flash of blue stars.

Princess Winsome stood there astonished. This task of spinning would take up most of her waking hours for the next three weeks. Turning to the wheel, she arranged the silk around the spindle and the wheel with more hope than she'd had an hour before. As she spun, words popped into her head from she knew not where to a tune she had never heard before.

> *My godmother bade me spin*
> *So that my heart may not be sad*
> *I'll spin and sing for my brother's sake.*
> *And the spinning makes me glad.*
> *Spin and whir, the wheel goes round*
> *So my brother won't suffer harm,*
> *The fairy pearl flute shall be found,*
> *And I'll break the charm.*
>
> *Spin, sing, my golden thread,*
> *So that my heart won't be sad,*
> *I'll spin and sing for my brother's sake,*
> *And the spinning makes me glad.*
> *Spin, sing, my golden thread,*
> *In the moon's bright ray.*
> *The spinning wheel my grief shall heal,*
> *For love will find a way.*

As she sang, she grew happier, and the night seemed not terrifying but warm and welcome—an evening with a sweet and creamy feel to it as the soft wind played through the plum trees. Then she heard a rustle at her window and rushed to the small opening in the stone wall. Reaching out over the sill, she found a white dove carrying a message in its beak. She read:

> *Fairest princess, don't despair,*
> *For I am coming soon,*
> *As soon as I find the flute of pearl*
> *Before the next full moon.*
> *But just to let me know that you*
> *Got to read this note,*
> *Send me a token with the dove—*
> *Like the chain about your throat.*

On it, I've heard it said, you had
A heart of emerald green.
On my shield I'll fasten it
So that it may be seen.
Once seeing it, all foes must yield
To me that very day.
Very soon I'll come to rescue you,
For love will find a way.

Who might her rescuer be? Princess Winsome wondered. She took the emerald from around her neck and fastened it to the dove's wing. The bird flew away in the moonlight and the sight was so lovely, another song came unbidden to her lips:

Now, flutter and fly, flutter and fly,
Bear him my precious heart,
Be a brave little carrier dove,
And I'll take my silk and start.
Tell him I'm at my spinning wheel,
Singing as it turns and hums,
Waiting the slow, tedious days—
Waiting until he comes.

Spin, sing, my golden thread,
So that my heart won't be sad.
I'll spin and sing for my brother's sake,
And the spinning makes me glad.
Spin, sing, my golden thread,
In the moon's bright ray.
The spinning wheel my grief shall heal,
For love will find a way.

Worn out by so many strange events, the exhausted girl slept. At dawn she rose to spin while the chow chow dozed at her feet. She heard a noise and saw someone had slipped a plate of rice underneath the door. Looking closer, she smiled, for this rice had fish mixed with it.

Her morning passed industriously until there came a knock at her window at midday. A petaled head peeked through, and to the princess' astonishment, her visitor was a flower-shaped fairy, dressed like a blue chrysanthemum. She asked the flower what it wanted. It replied:

> *This morning, fair princess, I was sleeping*
> *As the dawn flushed the sky,*
> *And then I heard the sweet racket*
> *Of a warrior passing by.*
> *He stopped and plucked me from my stem,*
> *"Chrysanthemum," said he,*
> *"Will you be my messenger today?*
> *Tell Winsome she will be free."*

"Thank you, sweet flower," the princess replied. "You must have traveled a ways to bring me such a message. You've brightened my day. I see that this mysterious suitor wishes to win my heart slowly by a hint here and there. Very well.

> *Tell him I'm at my spinning wheel,*
> *Singing as it turns and hums,*
> *Waiting the slow and tedious days—*
> *Waiting until he comes.*

The following day, she was petting the dog during a break from her spinning. By this time, her brother had gotten restless and was tiring of his four legs and heavy fur coat. To humor him, Princess Winsome was tossing about a tiny ball of spun silk, and he was chasing it about the small room, when there came a knock at the window. Over the sill peeked the silky white face of a water lily. Its tiny green legs were curled beneath its lovely, outstretched white petals which framed its face like a wreath. The flower began to chant a song:

> *I come from your faithful warrior.*
> *He plucked me from my pad,*
> *Saying, "Get thee to the princess,*
> *So she won't be sad."*
> *So, here I am, to remind you to hope,*
> *Do not give in to despair.*
> *Return to spinning at your wheel*
> *That golden thread so fair.*

The princess laughed with pleasure and gave the flower a kiss. She replied:

Tell him I'm at my spinning wheel,
Singing as it turns and hums,
Waiting the slow, tedious days—
Waiting until he comes.

The third day, toward evening, yet another knock came at the door. When the princess opened it, she saw a lone red poppy on the floor. The bedraggled thing was obviously so thirsty that Winsome grabbed a glass of water and plunked the poppy in it. In an hour, the flower had more than recovered and was glowing a soft, red color.

"How lovely you look!" the princess said. "I'm sure everyone must compliment you."

"They do, but I never boast of my looks," the poppy replied. "Remember, the nail that sticks out the most gets hammered. But your warrior liked my color. He spotted me soon after he had fought in battle. He wanted to let you know that his victory was due to your jeweled heart on his shield.

He saw me blushing beside a wall,
Glistening in the sun
With pleasure, having just seen how
His battle had been won.
"You're a witness!" he cried, and gave me a kiss,
And sent me on my way
To tell you how valor and purity
Won his battle for you today.

Then the poppy snoozed off, for she had a long day. Six more days passed, and the princess stayed faithful to the task that her godmother had given her. The ball of spun silk was growing larger and the bundle of silk was getting smaller. Meanwhile, the poppy, the water lily, and the chrysanthemum had slipped into the moist earth below the tower to spy out whatever activities the Tiger Lady and her jade dragon were involved in. At least they were feeding their prisoners regularly, and for that, Winsome was glad.

One evening, Princess Winsome heard at her window a peck from a nightingale. She looked out and saw the famous bird bearing a gift in its beak. It was a fragrant lotus flower which began to speak in low, melodious tones:

> *Fair princess, do not give up yet,*
> *For I saw two days ago*
> *A brave warrior drinking from a stream*
> *Made cold by mountain snow.*
> *When he saw me standing there,*
> *He said, "O kind, wise flower,*
> *Would you mind if a bird took you in its beak*
> *To the princess this very hour?"*
>
> *Well, it took us two days to find you,*
> *And we must be going along,*
> *Except that the nightingale desires*
> *To sing an original song.*
>
> *Princess, princess*, the nightingale sang,
> *You must consider it true*
> *That you're not forgotten, heaven's on your side,*
> *And love is coming to you.*

"Why, thank you," said the princess, "for the new moon is upon us and I was about to give way to despair. It is a full two weeks since that horrible day when we were kidnapped. If you see the warrior:

> *Tell him I'm at my spinning wheel,*
> *Singing as it turns and hums,*
> *Waiting the slow, tedious days—*
> *Waiting until he comes.*

A few nights later, the princess awoke with a start. The chow chow was sleeping soundly, but the princess was sure she heard something outside crawling about the ground. In the darkness, she could not see what the scurrying below her window could be. So she waited until daylight and once again looked out the window to a scene twenty feet below her. Then she laughed. Huddled in sleep was a black-and-white furry panda curled up beside a pile of plum tree branches. Looking up at her from the tree was a beautiful plum blossom. It said:

This panda was in a forest glade,
Ready to eat bamboo,
When up should walk this warrior
Who only spoke of you.
And so the panda hurried down here,
And soon he'll awake to say
That your warrior draws nearer and nearer,
Speaking of you night and day.

The princess was overjoyed. Surely her rescuer was getting closer.

She needed such encouragement from her furry visitor, for yet another week passed before the sixth flowery messenger arrived. The princess had been restless all day, for at home she was used to running about. Here she could only walk a few steps before she bumped into a wall. She noticed her brother was losing interest in life. He was eating less and less each day, and his beautiful fur was becoming matted with dust, as she had no way to clean him. No longer did he lick her face with his large, blue tongue. When she saw the daisy peeking into her window in the late afternoon shadows, she began to cry. The flower softly sang to her:

You should know, O princess,
I was standing in the sun
When this warrior took me in his hand,
Counting petals one by one.

He said, "O daisy white and gold,
The princess must count these too.
By your petals she shall finally learn
If my ambitious quest is through—
Whether or not her champion has found
The precious pearl flute he sought."
So, many miles from the Great Wall
His token I have brought.

"Must I pluck you?" asked the princess. "Let me see," she said, taking the daisy in her hand. "Let's see what today has brought: he's found it, found it not, found it, found it not."

Round and round she turned the flower as she picked each white petal. "He's found it," she said, "found it not, found it, found it not." Then there were but three more petals left. "He's found it," she said, and then, "found it not . . . he's found it! O sweet Wisdom," she said to the dog by her side, "we're saved, we're saved, we're saved! Only one more night in this horrible place! And to think I only have a few more hours of spinning left." She quickly went to the wheel and sang:

> *O spinning wheel, spinning wheel,*
> *Reel your thread today.*
> *We'll soon be free and I'll be a bride,*
> *For love has found a way.*

That night, rays from a half-moon poured though the little window as the princess and prince slept, she with her head upon his furry coat. The next morning, she heard a sound she'd never heard before. It was the sound of a flute playing. She looked down into the orchard to see a man standing there in bright red clothes holding a flute made of some shimmery substance. So this was the flute of pearl, she thought.

"Lean out your window, sweet Winsome," he called to her. "Rescuers are at hand. Listen, as on this priceless flute I call the fairies to a tryst. They will arrive here in rainbow bubbles."

He began to play a sweet melody on the flute, and to Winsome's delight, she glimpsed colored globes floating through the air. Tiny voices were coming from within them, singing:

> *To the aid of the gallant warrior,*
> *To the help of the princess fair,*
> *To the rescue of the chow chow,*
> *We have come to the dragon's lair.*
> *And now at your request,*
> *We pause in our bright array*
> *To end your weary quest,*
> *For love has found a way.*

Floating in the largest bubble of all was the godmother, dressed in peach robes with a crown of stars on her head. Gathering the other fairies about her, she paused to face Princess Winsome.

"I bade you spin many skeins of silken thread," Lady Qing said. "If you obeyed me faithfully, then you will have pleased eternity. What have you to show for your three weeks of work in your prison?"

"Only this, O Godmother," said Winsome, holding up a mammoth silken ball.

As I sang and worked and sang and worked,
At last I wound it all
Until the silk all golden
Rolled into this wonder ball.

The godmother smiled and beckoned. "Your future husband stands here down below, so drop the ball into his hands."

Winsome dropped the ball down many feet to the waiting crowd. Catching it, the warrior bowed. Turning to the fairies, who had climbed out of their bubbles and were fluttering about the orchard, he tossed the ball to them. The ball flew from one to the other, and in a minute it had become unraveled, causing a web of golden thread to blanket the orchard.

Suddenly, as if woken from sleep, the Tiger Lady and the dragon burst upon the scene. In a twinkling, they were caught in the golden web like flies for a spider. The fairies again began to sing:

We came, we came at your call,
To the help of the princess fair,
To the rescue of the chow chow,
We came to the dragon's lair.
We came, we came at your call,
These fearsome two to quell.
And now they both must humbly bow
To the might of the fairies' spell.
Love's golden thread can bind
The fiercest dragon's threat.
And the Tiger Lady's schemes
Haven't hurt us yet.

The dragon and the Tiger Lady glowered at the crowd, helpless as they were enmeshed in golden thread. The warrior drew his sword, released the dragon, and demanded the key to the tower. Receiving it, he unlocked the lower door and sped up the winding stair to the room where the princess and chow chow awaited. Sweeping the princess into his arms and planting a kiss on her cheek, he carried her and led the dog down into the bright sunlight. A cheer rose from the crowd.

Then the warrior drew his sword and approached the glowering Tiger Lady, demanding to know how to turn the dog into a boy again.

She shook her head, and the warrior hesitated, loath to attack a woman.

"Play your flute," Winsome suggested.

He put the instrument to his mouth and out came the same tunes that the princess had been singing in her tower these three weeks. As he played, the woman dropped to her hands and knees, her eyes grew larger, her body grew longer and covered with fur. As the astonished crowd of fairies and humans watched, she grew a tail, whiskers sprouted by her mouth, and stripes covered her everywhere. A tiger crouched before the warrior.

"Leave us forever," he said, "and go live in the mountains." The tigress bounded off through the trees and across the plains that led to the far-off snow-covered peaks.

Fearing for his life, the dragon began to speak.

"You must pick seven silver plums," he said, "to turn your dog back into a prince. Only now that I have told you the truth, spare my life."

At once Princess Winsome plucked the plums, and presented them to the chow chow, who swallowed them. Slowly his fur turned to skin, the large, black eyes became brown, the blue tongue became a human mouth, and Prince Wisdom came into view. He bowed low to the warrior and said:

> *Wherever you go and whatever you do,*
> *Warrior pure and true,*
> *The favors of our kingdom shall*
> *Be richly showered on you.*
> *And thank you, Fairy Godmother,*
> *And fairies, rainbow-hued,*
> *I lack the words, but not the feeling,*

Of deepest gratitude.
If ever the loyal service
Of a mortal you should need,
Prince Wisdom lives to serve you—
No matter what the deed.

As for you, O bravest sister,
Each day you spun and cried
Over our sad imprisonment,
When our freedom was denied.
But now your reward stands, waiting here.
Because of your tenacity,
Soon you shall be a royal bride,
Having pleased eternity.

The princess clapped. "My spoiled brother has disappeared forever," she said, "and in his place is someone who has learned though suffering. And I would not have him back if it were not for the Jade Dragon, who told us how to set him free. Thank you," she said, stepping near the dragon to extend her blessing. The beast, who was sadly crouched next to one of the fairies, looked up as the shadow of her arm fell upon him. There was an explosion of purple stars, and before them all stood Lady Qing's long lost brother, Lord Jade, dressed in a green silk gown, with a long, silver beard.

The Lady Qing stood there speechless, for fifty years had passed since the greatest sorrow of her childhood. Lord Jade spoke, gesturing toward the astonished Princess Winsome. He said:

This we learned from a shadow of a tree
That sways to and fro on the wall—
That where the princess may never be,
Her influence does fall.
Someday her shadow shall unbind
The cruelest imprisonment of them all.

He threw himself to the ground in sorrow before his sister for all the misery he had caused people in the long years he had been a dragon.

But Lady Qing rushed to him and pulled him to his feet and embraced him. Smiling, Princess Winsome said, "Shall we not return to the palace where I may prepare for my wedding day on the Birthday of One Hundred Flowers?"

"It shall be done," said the Lady Qing. Three of the fairies invited the princess, prince, and warrior to share their bubbles. And as they all floated toward the palace by the Yellow Sea, they sang:

> *Love's cord has bound*
> *The dragon's arm,*
> *Turned him back into a man,*
> *Released the evil charm.*
> *As Princess Winsome becomes*
> *Wed to the warrior today,*
> *We fairies one and all*
> *No longer need to stay.*
>
> *Evil is defeated,*
> *Our champion has won his bride.*
> *Rejoicing in our victory,*
> *We'll drift on the ocean's tide.*
> *Our rainbow bubbles bright,*
> *Will help us float away.*
> *All wrong has been set right,*
> *For love has found a way!*

Printed in the United States
107798LV00007B/439-486/A